James Thomson

Winter

James Thomson

Winter

ISBN/EAN: 9783337257019

Printed in Europe, USA, Canada, Australia, Japan

Cover: Foto ©Andreas Hilbeck / pixelio.de

More available books at **www.hansebooks.com**

WINTER

BY

JAMES THOMSON

ILLUSTRATED

𝔅oston

ESTES AND LAURIAT

PUBLISHERS

Typography by J. S. Cushing & Co., Boston.

Presswork by Berwick & Smith, Boston.

WINTER.

SEE, Winter comes to rule the varied year,
   Sullen and sad, with all his rising train ;
Vapours, and clouds, and storms. Be these
     my theme ;
These, that exalt the soul to solemn thought
And heavenly musing. Welcome, kindred
     glooms !

Congenial horrors, hail! with frequent foot,
Pleased have I, in my cheerful morn of life,
When nursed by careless solitude I lived,
And sung of Nature with unceasing joy,
Pleased have I wandered through your rough
    domain ;
Trod the pure virgin snows, myself as pure ;
Heard the winds roar, and the big torrent
    burst ;
Or seen the deep-fermenting tempest brewed,
In the grim evening sky. Thus passed the
    time,
Till through the lucid chambers of the south
Looked out the joyous Spring, looked out, and
    smiled.
    To thee, the patron of this first essay,
The Muse, O Wilmington! renews her song.
Since has she rounded the revolving year :
Skimmed the gay Spring; on eagle-pinions
    borne,
Attempted through the Summer-blaze to rise ;
Then swept o'er Autumn with the shadowy
    gale ;
And now among the wintry clouds again,

8

Rolled in the doubling storm, she tries to
    soar;
To swell her note with all the rushing winds;
To suit her sounding cadence to the floods;
As is her theme, her numbers wildly great:
Thrice happy could she fill thy judging ear
With bold description, and with manly
    thought.
Nor art thou skilled in awful schemes alone,
And how to make a mighty people thrive;
But equal goodness, sound integrity,
A firm, unshaken, uncorrupted soul
Amid a sliding age; and, burning strong,
Not vainly blazing, for thy country's weal.
A steady spirit regularly free —
These, each exalting each, the statesman
    light
Into the patriot; these, the public hope
And eye to thee converting, bid the Muse
Record what envy dares not flattery call.
    Now when the cheerless empire of the
    sky
To Capricorn the Centaur-Archer yields,
And fierce Aquarius stains the inverted year;

9

Hung o'er the farthest verge of heaven, the
    sun
Scarce spreads o'er ether the dejected day.
Faint are his gleams, and ineffectual shoot
His struggling rays, in horizontal lines,
Through the thick air; as, clothed in cloudy
    storm,
Weak, wan, and broad, he skirts the southern
    sky:
And, soon-descending, to the long dark night,
Wide-shading all, the prostrate world resigns.
Nor is the night unwished; while vital heat,
Light, life, and joy, the dubious day forsake.
Meantime, in sable cincture, shadows vast,
Deep-tinged and damp, and congregated
    clouds,
And all the vapoury turbulence of heaven,
Involve the face of things. Thus Winter
    falls,
A heavy gloom oppressive o'er the world,
Through Nature shedding influence malign,
And rouses up the seeds of dark disease.
The soul of man dies in him, loathing life,
And black with more than melancholy views.

The cattle droop; and o'er the furrowed land,
Fresh from the plough, the dun-discoloured
      flocks,
Untended spreading, crop the wholesome root.
Along the woods, along the moorish fens,
Sighs the sad genius of the coming storm;
And up among the loose disjointed cliffs,
And fractured mountains wild, the brawling
      brook
And cave, presageful, send a hollow moan,
Resounding long in listening Fancy's ear.
   Then comes the father of the tempest forth,
Wrapt in black glooms. First joyless rains
      obscure
Drive through the mingling skies with vapour
      foul;
Dash on the mountain's brow, and shake the
      woods,
That grumbling wave below. The unsightly
      plain
Lies a brown deluge; as the low-bent clouds
Pour flood on flood, yet unexhausted still
Combine, and deepening into night, shut up
The day's fair face. The wanderers of heaven,

Each to his home, retire ; save those that love
To take their pastime in the troubled air,
Or skimming flutter round the dimply pool ;
The cattle from the untasted fields return,
And ask, with meaning low, their wonted
    stalls,
Or ruminate in the contiguous shade.
Thither the household feathery people crowd,
The crested cock, with all his female train,
Pensive and dripping ; while the cottage-hind
Hangs o'er the enlivening blaze, and taleful
    there
Recounts his simple frolic : much he talks,
And much he laughs, nor recks the storm
    that blows
Without, and rattles on his humble roof.
  Wide o'er the brim, with many a torrent
    swelled,
And the mixed ruin of its banks o'erspread,
At last the roused-up river pours along :
Resistless, roaring, dreadful, down it comes,
From the rude mountain, and the mossy wild,
Tumbling through rocks abrupt, and sound-
    ing far ;

Then o'er the sanded valley floating spreads,
Calm, sluggish, silent; till again, constrained
Between two meeting hills, it bursts away,
Where rocks and woods o'erhang the turbid
    stream ;

There gathering triple force, rapid and deep,
It boils and wheels and foams and thunders
    through.
  Nature! great parent! whose unceasing
    hand   15

Rolls round the seasons of the changeful
    year,
How mighty, how majestic, are thy works!
With what a pleasing dread they swell the
    soul,
That sees astonished, and astonished sings!
Ye too, ye winds, that now begin to blow
With boisterous sweep, I raise my voice to
    you.
Where are your stores, ye powerful beings!
    say,
Where your aerial magazines, reserved
To swell the brooding terrors of the storm?
In what far distant region of the sky,
Hushed in deep silence, sleep you when 't is
    calm?
    When from the pallid sky the Sun descends
With many a spot, that o'er his glaring orb,
Uncertain wanders, stained ; red fiery streaks
Begin to flush around.   The reeling clouds
Stagger with dizzy poise, as doubting yet
Which master to obey : while rising slow,
Blank, in the leaden-coloured east, the Moon
Wears a wan circle round her blunted horns.

Seen through the turbid fluctuating air,
The stars obtuse emit a shivering ray;
Or frequent seem to shoot athwart the gloom,
And long behind them trail the whitening
    blaze.
Snatched in short eddies, plays the withered
    leaf;
And on the flood the dancing feather floats.
With broadened nostrils to the sky upturned,
The conscious heifer snuffs the stormy gale.
E'en as the matron, at her nightly task,
With pensive labour draws the flaxen thread,
The wasted taper and the crackling flame
Foretell the blast.   But chief the plumy race,
The tenants of the sky, its changes speak.
Retiring from the downs, where all day long
They picked their scanty fare, a blackening
    train
Of clamorous rooks thick urge their weary
    ·   flight,
And seek the closing shelter of the grove.
Assiduous, in his bower, the wailing owl
Plies his sad song.   The cormorant on high
Wheels from the deep, and screams along the
    land.   17

Loud shrieks the soaring hern; and with wild
  wing
The circling seafowl cleave the flaky clouds.
Ocean, unequal pressed, with broken tide
And blind commotion heaves; while from the
  shore,
Eat into caverns by the restless wave,
And forest-rustling mountain, comes a voice,
That solemn-sounding bids the world prepare.
Then issues forth the storm with sudden
  burst,
And hurls the whole precipitated air
Down in a torrent.   On the passive main
Descends the ethereal force, and with strong
  gust
Turns from its bottom the discoloured deep.
Through the black night, that sits immense
  around,
Lashed into foam, the fierce conflicting brine
Seems o'er a thousand raging waves to burn.
Meantime the mountain-billows, to the clouds
In dreadful tumult swelled, surge above surge,
Burst into chaos with tremendous roar,
And anchored navies from their stations drive,

Wild as the winds across the howling waste
Of mighty waters: now the inflated wave
Straining they scale, and now impetuous shoot
Into the secret chambers of the deep,
The wintry Baltic thundering o'er their head.
Emerging thence again, before the breath
Of full exerted heaven they wing their course,
And dart on distant coasts; if some sharp
    rock,
Or shoal insidious break not their career,
And in loose fragments fling them floating
    round.
  Nor less at land the loosened tempest
    reigns.
The mountain thunders; and its sturdy sons
Stoop to the bottom of the rocks they shade.
Lone on the midnight steep, and all aghast,
The dark wayfaring stranger breathless toils,
And, often falling, climbs against the blast.
Low waves the rooted forest, vexed, and
    sheds
What of its tarnished honours yet remain;
Dashed down, and scattered, by the tearing
    wind's

Assiduous fury, its gigantic limbs.
Thus struggling through the dissipated grove.
The whirling tempest raves along the plain;
And on the cottage thatched, or lordly roof,
Keen-fastening, shakes them to the solid
    base.
Sleep frighted flies; and round the rocking
    dome,
For entrance eager, howls the savage blast.
Then too, they say, through all the burdened
    air,
Long groans are heard, shrill sounds, and
    distant sighs,
That, uttered by the Demon of the night,
Warn the devoted wretch of woe and death.
    Huge uproar lords it wide. The clouds,
      commixed
With stars, swift gliding, sweep along the
    sky.
All Nature reels: till Nature's king, who oft
Amid tempestuous darkness dwells alone,
And on the wings of the careering wind
Walks dreadfully serene, commands a calm;
Then straight, air, sea, and earth are hushed
    at once.   22

As yet 't is midnight deep.   The weary
    clouds,
Slow meeting, mingle into solid gloom.
Now, while the drowsy world lies lost in
    sleep,
Let me associate with the serious Night,
And Contemplation, her sedate compeer;
Let me shake off the intrusive cares of day,
And lay the meddling senses all aside.
    Where now, ye lying vanities of life!
Ye ever tempting, ever cheating train!
Where are you now? and what is your
    amount?
Vexation, disappointment, and remorse:
Sad, sickening thought! and yet deluded man,
A scene of crude disjointed visions past,
And broken slumbers, rises still resolved,
With new-flushed hopes, to run the giddy
    round.
   · Father of light and life! thou Good Su-
    preme!
O teach me what is good! teach me thyself!
Save me from folly, vanity, and vice,
From every low pursuit! and feed my soul

With knowledge, conscious peace, and virtue
    pure —
Sacred, substantial, never-fading bliss!
  The keener tempests come: and fuming
    dun
From all the livid east, or piercing north,
Thick clouds ascend; in whose capacious
    womb
A vapoury deluge lies, to snow congealed.
Heavy they roll their fleecy world along;
And the sky saddens with the gathered
    storm.
Through the hushed air the whitening shower
    descends,
At first thin wavering; till at last the flakes
Fall broad, and wide, and fast, dimming the
    day
With a continual flow. The cherished fields
Put on their winter-robe of purest white.
'T is brightness all; save where the new snow
    melts
Along the mazy current. Low the woods
Bow their hoar head; and ere the languid
    sun

24

Faint from the west emits its evening ray,
Earth's universal face, deep-hid and chill,
Is one wild dazzling waste, that buries wide

The works of man.   Drooping, the labourer-
ox
Stands covered o'er with snow, and then de-
mands

The fruit of all his toil. The fowls of heaven,
Tamed by the cruel season, crowd around
The winnowing store, and claim the little
    boon
Which Providence assigns them. One alone,
The redbreast, sacred to the household gods,
Wisely regardful of the embroiling sky,
In joyless fields and thorny thickets leaves
His shivering mates, and pays to trusted man
His annual visit. Half afraid, he first
Against the window beats ; then, brisk, alights
On the warm hearth ; then, hopping o'er the
    floor,
Eyes all the smiling family askance,
And pecks, and starts, and wonders where
    he is ;
Till more familiar grown, the table-crumbs
Attract his slender feet. The foodless wilds
Pour forth their brown inhabitants. The
    hare,
Though timorous of heart, and hard beset
By death in various forms, dark snares and
    dogs,
And more unpitying men, the garden seeks,

Urged on by fearless want.   The bleating
    kind
Eye the bleak heaven, and next the glistening
    earth,
With looks of dumb despair; then, sad dis-
    persed,
Dig for the withered herb through heaps of
    snow.
  Now, shepherds, to your helpless charge be
    kind,
Baffle the raging year, and fill their pens
With food at will; lodge them below the
    storm,
And watch them strict: for from the bellow-
    ing east,
In this dire season, oft the whirlwind's wing
Sweeps up the burden of whole wintry plains
In one wide waft, and o'er the hapless flocks,
Hid in the hollow of two neighbouring hills,
The billowy tempest whelms: till, upward
    urged,
The valley to a shining mountain swells,
Tipped with a wreath high-curling in the sky.
  As thus the snows arise, and, foul and fierce,

All Winter drives along the darkened air,
In his own loose-revolving fields, the swain
Disastered stands ; sees other hills ascend,
Of unknown joyless brow ; and other scenes,
Of horrid prospect, shag the trackless plain :
Nor finds the river, nor the forest, hid
Beneath the formless wild ; but wanders on
From hill to dale, still more and more astray ;
Impatient flouncing through the drifted heaps,
Stung with the thoughts of home ; the
    thoughts of home
Rush on his nerves, and call their vigour
    forth
In many a vain attempt. How sinks his soul!
What black despair, what horror fills his
    heart!
When for the dusky spot, which fancy feigned
His tufted cottage, rising through the snow,
He meets the roughness of the middle waste,
Far from the track and blessed abode of
    man ;
While round him night resistless closes fast,
And every tempest, howling o'er his head,
Renders the savage wilderness more wild.

Then throng the busy shapes into his mind,
Of covered pits, unfathomably deep,
A dire descent! beyond the power of frost;
Of faithless bogs; of precipices huge,
Smoothed up with snow; and, what is land
    unknown,
What water, of the still unfrozen spring,
In the loose marsh or solitary lake,
Where the fresh fountain from the bottom
    boils.
These check his fearful steps; and down he
    sinks,
Beneath the shelter of the shapeless drift,
Thinking o'er all the bitterness of death;
Mixed with the tender anguish nature shoots
Through the wrung bosom of the dying man,
His wife, his children, and his friends unseen.
In vain for him the officious wife prepares
The fire fair-blazing, and the vestment warm;
In vain his little children, peeping out
Into the mingling storm, demand their sire,
With tears of artless innocence. Alas!
Nor wife, nor children more shall he behold,
Nor friends, nor sacred home. On every
    nerve   33

The deadly winter seizes; shuts up sense;
And, o'er his inmost vitals creeping cold,
Lays him along the snows, a stiffened corse,
Stretched out, and bleaching in the northern
    blast.
  Ah! little think the gay licentious proud,
Whom pleasure, power, and affluence sur-
    round;
They who their thoughtless hours in giddy
    mirth,
And wanton, often cruel, riot waste;
Ah! little think they, while they dance along,
How many feel, this very moment, death,
And all the sad variety of pain.
How many sink in the devouring flood,
Or more devouring flame. How many bleed,
By shameful variance betwixt man and man.
How many pine in want, and dungeon-
    glooms;
Shut from the common air, and common use
Of their own limbs. How many drink the
    cup
Of baleful grief, or eat the bitter bread
Of misery. Sore pierced by wintry winds,

How many shrink into the sordid hut
Of cheerless poverty. How many shake
With all the fiercer tortures of the mind,
Unbounded passion, madness, guilt, remorse ;
Whence tumbled headlong from the height
       of life,
They furnish matter for the tragic Muse.
Even in the vale, where wisdom loves to
       dwell,
With friendship, peace, and contemp'ation
       joined,
How many, racked with honest passions,
       droop
In deep retired distress. How many stand
Around the death-bed of their dearest friends,
And point the parting anguish. Thought
       fond man
Of these, and all the thousand nameless ills
That one incessant struggle render life,
One scene of toil, of suffering, and of fate,
Vice in his high career would stand appalled,
And heedless rambling Impulse learn to
       think ;
The conscious heart of Charity would warm,

And her wide wish Benevolence dilate;
The social tear would rise. the social sigh;
And into clear perfection. gradual bliss,
Refining still. the social passions work.
    And here can I forget the generous band,
Who, touched with human woe, redressive
    searched
Into the horrors of the gloomy jail —
Unpitied. and unheard, where Misery moans;
Where Sickness pines; where thirst and hun-
    ger burn,
And poor misfortune feels the lash of vice?
While in the land of liberty, the land
Whose every street and public meeting glow
With open freedom, little tyrants raged:
Snatched the lean morsel from the starving
    mouth;
Tore from cold wintry limbs the tattered
    weed;
Even robbed them of the last of comforts,
    sleep;
The free-born Briton to the dungeon chained,
Or. as the lust of cruelty prevailed,
At pleasure marked him with inglorious
    stripes;   36

And crushed out lives, by secret barbarous
    ways,
That for their country would have toiled or
    bled.

O great design! if executed well,
With patient care, and wisdom-tempered zeal.
Ye sons of mercy! yet resume the search;
Drag forth the legal monsters into light.
Wrench from their hands oppression's iron
    rod,   37

And bid the cruel feel the pains they give.
Much still untouched remains; in this rank
    age,
Much is the patriot's weeding hand required.
The toils of law (what dark insidious men
Have cumbrous added to perplex the truth,
And lengthen simple justice into trade),
How glorious were the day that saw these
    broke,
And every man within the reach of right!

By wintry famine roused, from all the tract
Of horrid mountains which the shining Alps,
And wavy Apennines, and Pyrenees,
Branch out stupendous into distant lands,
Cruel as death, and hungry as the grave,
Burning for blood, bony and gaunt and grim,
Assembling wolves in raging troops descend;
And, pouring o'er the country, bear along,
Keen as the north-wind sweeps the glossy
    snow.
All is their prize. They fasten on the steed,
Press him to earth, and pierce his mighty
    heart.
Nor can the bull his awful front defend,

Or shake the murdering savages away.
Rapacious, at the mother's throat they fly,
And tear the screaming infant from her
    breast.
The godlike face of man avails him naught.
Even beauty, force divine! at whose bright
    glance
The generous lion stands in softened gaze,
Here bleeds, a hapless undistinguished prey.
But if, apprised of the severe attack,
The country be shut up, lured by the scent,
On churchyards drear (inhuman to relate!)
The disappointed prowlers fall, and dig
The shrouded body from the grave; o'er
    which,
Mixed with foul shades and frighted ghosts,
    they howl.
    Among those hilly regions, where, embraced
In peaceful vales the happy Grisons dwell,
Oft, rushing sudden from the loaded cliffs,
Mountains of snow their gathering terrors
    roll.
From steep to steep, loud-thundering, down
    they come,

A wintry waste in dire commotion all:
And herds, and flocks, and travellers, and
    swains,
And sometimes whole brigades of marching
    troops,
Or hamlets sleeping in the dead of night,
Are deep beneath the smothering ruin
    whelmed.
  Now, all amid the rigours of the year,
In the wild depth of Winter, while, without,
The ceaseless winds blow ice, be my retreat
Between the groaning forest and the shore,
Beat by the boundless multitude of waves,
A rural, sheltered, solitary scene:
Where ruddy fire and beaming tapers join
To cheer the gloom. There studious let me
    sit,
And hold high converse with the mighty
    dead;
Sages of ancient time, as gods revered,
As gods beneficent, who blessed mankind
With arts, and arms, and humanised a world.
Roused at the inspiring thought, I throw aside
The long-lived volume; and, deep-musing,
    hail

The sacred shades, that, slowly rising, pass
Before my wondering eyes.   First Socrates,
Who, firmly good in a corrupted state,
Against the rage of tyrants single stood,
Invincible : calm reason's holy law,
That voice of God within the attentive mind,
Obeying, fearless, or in life, or death :
Great moral teacher!   Wisest of mankind!
Solon the next, who built his commonweal
On equity's wide base : by tender laws
A lively people curbing, yet undamped
Preserving still that quick peculiar fire,
Whence in the laurelled field of finer arts
And of bold freedom, they unequalled shone —
The pride of smiling Greece, and human-kind.
Lycurgus then, who bowed beneath the force
Of strictest discipline, severely wise,
All human passions.   Following him, I see,
As at Thermopylæ he glorious fell,
The firm devoted chief, who proved by deeds
The hardest lesson which the other taught.
Then Aristides lifts his honest front :
Spotless of heart, to whom the unflattering
    voice

Of Freedom gave the noblest name of Just;
In pure majestic poverty revered:
Who, even his glory to his country's weal
Submitting, swelled a haughty rival's fame.
Reared by his care, of softer ray appears
Cimon, sweet-souled: whose genius, rising
      strong,
Shook off the load of young debauch: abroad
The scourge of Persian pride, at home the
      friend
Of every worth and every splendid art;
Modest, and simple, in the pomp of wealth.
Then the last worthies of declining Greece.
Late called to glory, in unequal times,
Pensive appear. The fair Corinthian boast,
Timoleon, tempered happy, mild and firm,
Who wept the brother while the tyrant bled:
And, equal to the best, the Theban Pair,
Whose virtues, in heroic concord joined,
Their country raised to freedom, empire,
      fame:
He too, with whom Athenian honour sunk,
And left a mass of sordid lees behind —
Phocion the Good: in public life severe,

To virtue still inexorably firm :
But when, beneath his low illustrious roof,
Sweet peace and happy wisdom smoothed his
    brow
Not friendship softer was, nor love more
    kind :
And he, the last of old Lycurgus' sons,
The generous victim to that vain attempt,
To save a rotten state, Agis, who saw
Even Sparta's self to servile avarice sunk.
The two Achaian heroes close the train :
Aratus, who awhile relumed the soul
Of fondly lingering liberty in Greece ;
And he, her darling, as her latest hope,
The gallant Philopœmen ; who to arms
Turned the luxurious pomp he could not cure ;
Or toiling in his farm, a simple swain ;
Or, bold and skilful, thundering in the field.
    Of rougher front, a mighty people come,
A race of heroes! in those virtuous times
Which knew no stain, save that with partial
    flame
Their dearest country they too fondly loved.
Her better founder first, the light of Rome,

Numa, who softened her rapacious sons:
Servius the king, who laid the solid base
On which o'er earth the vast republic spread.
Then the great consuls venerable rise:
The public father who the private quelled,
As on the dread tribunal sternly sad:
He whom his thankless country could not
       lose,
Camillus, only vengeful to her foes;
Fabricius, scorner of all-conquering gold;
And Cincinnatus, awful from the plough:
Thy willing victim, Carthage, bursting loose
From all that pleading Nature could oppose,
From a whole city's tears, by rigid faith
Imperious called, and honour's dire command;
Scipio, the gentle chief, humanely brave,
Who soon the race of spotless glory ran,
And, warm in youth, to the poetic shade
With friendship and philosophy retired;
Tully, whose powerful eloquence awhile
Restrained the rapid fate of rushing Rome;
Unconquered Cato, virtuous in extreme;
And thou, unhappy Brutus, kind of heart,
Whose steady arm, by awful virtue urged,

Lifted the Roman steel against thy friend.
Thousands, besides, the tribute of a verse
Demand; but who can count the stars of
    heaven?
Who sing their influence on this lower world?
  Behold, who yonder comes! in sober state,
Fair, mild, and strong, as is a vernal sun:
'T is Phœbus' self, or else the Mantuan swain.
Great Homer too appears, of daring wing,
Parent of song! and equal by his side,
The British Muse: joined hand in hand they
    walk,
Darkling, full up the middle steep to fame.
Nor absent are those shades, whose skilful
    touch
Pathetic drew the impassioned heart, and
    charmed
Transported Athens with the moral scene;
Nor those who, tuneful, waked the enchanting
    lyre.
  First of your kind! society divine!
Still visit thus my nights, for you reserved,
And mount my soaring soul to thoughts like
    yours.

Silence, thou lonely power, the door be thine!
See on the hallowed hour that none intrude,
Save a few chosen friends, who sometimes
    deign
To bless my humble roof, with sense refined,
Learning digested well, exalted faith,
Unstudied wit, and humour ever gay.
Or from the Muses' hill will Pope descend,
To raise the sacred hour, to bid it smile,
And with the social spirit warm the heart?
For though not sweeter his own Homer sings,
Yet is his life the more endearing song.
    Where art thou, Hammond? thou, the
    darling pride,
The friend and lover of the tuneful throng.
Ah why, dear youth, in all the blooming prime
Of vernal genius, where disclosing fast
Each active worth, each manly virtue lay,
Why wert thou ravished from our hope so
    soon?
What now avails that noble thirst of fame
Which stung thy fervent breast? that treasured
    store
Of knowledge early gained? that eager zeal

To serve thy country, glowing in the band
Of youthful patriots, who sustain her name?
What now, alas! that life-diffusing charm
Of sprightly wit? that rapture for the Muse,
That heart of friendship, and that soul of joy,
Which bade with softest light thy virtues
    smile?
Ah! only showed, to check our fond pursuits,
And teach our humbled hopes that life is
    vain!
  Thus in some deep retirement would I pass
The winter-glooms, with friends of pliant
    soul,
Or blithe, or solemn, as the theme inspired:
With them would search, if Nature's bound-
    less frame
Was called, late-rising from the void of
    night,
Or sprung eternal from the eternal mind;
Its life, its laws, its progress, and its end.
Hence larger prospects of the beauteous
    whole
Would, gradual, open on our opening minds;
And each diffusive harmony unite

In full perfection, to the astonished eye.
Then would we try to scan the moral world,
Which, though to us it seems embroiled,
    moves on
In higher order; fitted and impelled
By Wisdom's finest hand, and issuing all
In general good.   The sage historic Muse
Should next conduct us through the deeps of
    time :
Show us how empire grew, declined, and fell,
In scattered states; what makes the nations
    smile,
Improves their soil, and gives them double
    suns ;
And why they pine beneath the brightest
    skies,
In Nature's richest lap.   As thus we talked,
Our hearts would burn within us, would
    inhale
That portion of divinity, that ray
Of purest heaven, which lights the public
    soul
Of patriots and of heroes.   But if doomed,
In powerless humble fortune, to repress

These ardent risings of the kindling soul;
Then, even superior to ambition, we
Would learn the private virtues; how to
    glide

Through shades and plains, along the smooth-
    est stream
Of rural life: or, snatched away by hope,
Through the dim spaces of futurity.
With earnest eye anticipate those scenes

53

Of happiness and wonder, where the mind,
In endless growth and infinite ascent,
Rises from state to state, and world to world.
But when with these the serious thought is
      foiled,
We, shifting for relief, would play the shapes
Of frolic fancy; and incessant form
Those rapid pictures, that assembled train
Of fleet ideas, never joined before,
Whence lively wit excites to gay surprise;
Or folly-painting Humour, grave himself,
Calls laughter forth, deep-shaking every
      nerve.
  Meantime the village rouses up the fire;
While well attested, and as well believed,
Heard solemn, goes the goblin story round;
Till superstitious horror creeps o'er all.
Or, frequent in the sounding hall, they wake
The rural gambol. Rustic mirth goes round;
The simple joke that takes the shepherd's
      heart,
Easily pleased; the long loud laugh, sincere;
The kiss, snatched hasty from the side-long
      maid,

On purpose guardless, or pretending sleep;
The leap, the slap, the haul: and, shook to
    notes
Of native music, the respondent dance.
Thus jocund fleets with them the Winter-
    night.
  The city swarms intense. The public
    haunt,
Full of each theme and warm with mixed dis-
    course,
Hums indistinct. The sons of riot flow
Down the loose stream of false enchanted
    joy,
To swift destruction. On the rankled soul
The gaming fury falls; and in one gulf
Of total ruin, honour, virtue, peace,
Friends, families, and fortune, headlong sink.
Upsprings the dance along the lighted dome,
Mixed and evolved a thousand sprightly ways;
The glittering court effuses every pomp;
The circle deepens; beamed from gaudy
    robes,
Tapers, and sparkling gems, and radiant eyes,
A soft effulgence o'er the palace waves:

While, a gay insect in his summer-shine,
The fop, light fluttering, spreads his mealy
    wings.
    Dread o'er the scene, the ghost of Hamlet
    stalks ;
Othello rages ; poor Monimia mourns ;
And Belvidera pours her soul in love.
Terror alarms the breast ; the comely tear
Steals o'er the cheek : or else the comic Muse
Holds to the world a picture of itself,
And raises sly the fair impartial laugh.
Sometimes she lifts her strain, and paints the
    scenes.
Of beauteous life ; whate'er can deck man-
    kind,
Or charm the heart, in generous Bevil showed.
    O Thou, whose wisdom, solid, yet refined,
Whose patriot-virtues, and consummate skill
To touch the finer springs that move the
    world.
Joined to whate'er the Graces can bestow,
And all Apollo's animating fire,
Give thee, with pleasing dignity, to shine
At once the guardian, ornament, and joy,

Of polished life; permit the rural Muse.
O Chesterfield, to grace with thee her song!
Ere to the shades again she humbly flies,
Indulge her fond ambition, in thy train
(For every Muse has in thy train a place),
To mark thy various full-accomplished mind:
To mark that spirit, which, with British scorn,
Rejects the allurements of corrupted power;
That elegant politeness, which excels,
Even in the judgment of presumptuous France,
The boasted manners of her shining court;
That wit, the vivid energy of sense,
The truth of Nature, which, with Attic point
And kind well-tempered satire, smoothly keen,
Steals through the soul, and without pain
        corrects.
Or, rising thence, with yet a brighter flame,
O let me hail thee on some glorious day,
When to the listening senate, ardent, crowd
Britannia's sons to hear her pleaded cause.
Then dressed by thee, more amiably fair,
Truth the soft robe of mild persuasion wears;
Thou to assenting reason giv'st again
Her own enlightened thoughts; called from
        the heart, 59

The obedient passions on thy voice attend;
And even reluctant party feels awhile
Thy gracious power, as through the varied
  maze
Of eloquence, now smooth, now quick, now
  strong,
Profound and clear, you roll the copious
  flood.
  To thy loved haunt return, my happy
  Muse:
For now, behold, the joyous Winter days,
Frosty, succeed; and through the blue serene,
For sight too fine, the ethereal nitre flies;
Killing infectious damps, and the spent air
Storing afresh with elemental life.
Close crowds the shining atmosphere; and
  binds
Our strengthened bodies in its cold embrace,
Constringent; feeds, and animates our blood;
Refines our spirits, through the new-strung
  nerves,
In swifter sallies darting to the brain,
Where sits the soul, intense, collected, cool,
Bright as the skies, and as the season keen.

Winter.

All Nature feels the renovating force
Of Winter, only to the thoughtless eye
In ruin seen.   The frost-concocted glebe

Draws in abundant vegetable soul.
And gathers vigour for the coming year;
A stronger glow sits on the lively cheek
Of ruddy fire; and luculent along
The purer rivers flow, their sullen deeps,
Transparent, open to the shepherd's gaze,

And murmur hoarser at the fixing frost.
  What art thou, frost? and whence are thy
    keen stores
Derived, thou secret all-invading power,
Whom even the illusive fluid cannot fly?
Is not thy potent energy, unseen,
Myriads of little salts. or hooked, or shaped
Like double wedges. and diffused immense
Through water, earth, and ether? hence at
    eve,
Steamed eager from the red horizon round,
With the fierce rage of Winter deep suffused,
An icy gale. oft shifting, o'er the pool
Breathes a blue film. and in its mid career
Arrests the bickering stream. The loosened
    ice,
Let down the flood, and half dissolved by
    day,
Rustles no more ; but to the sedgy bank
Fast grows, or gathers round the pointed
    stone,
A crystal pavement, by the breath of Heaven
Cemented firm ; till. seized from shore to
    shore,

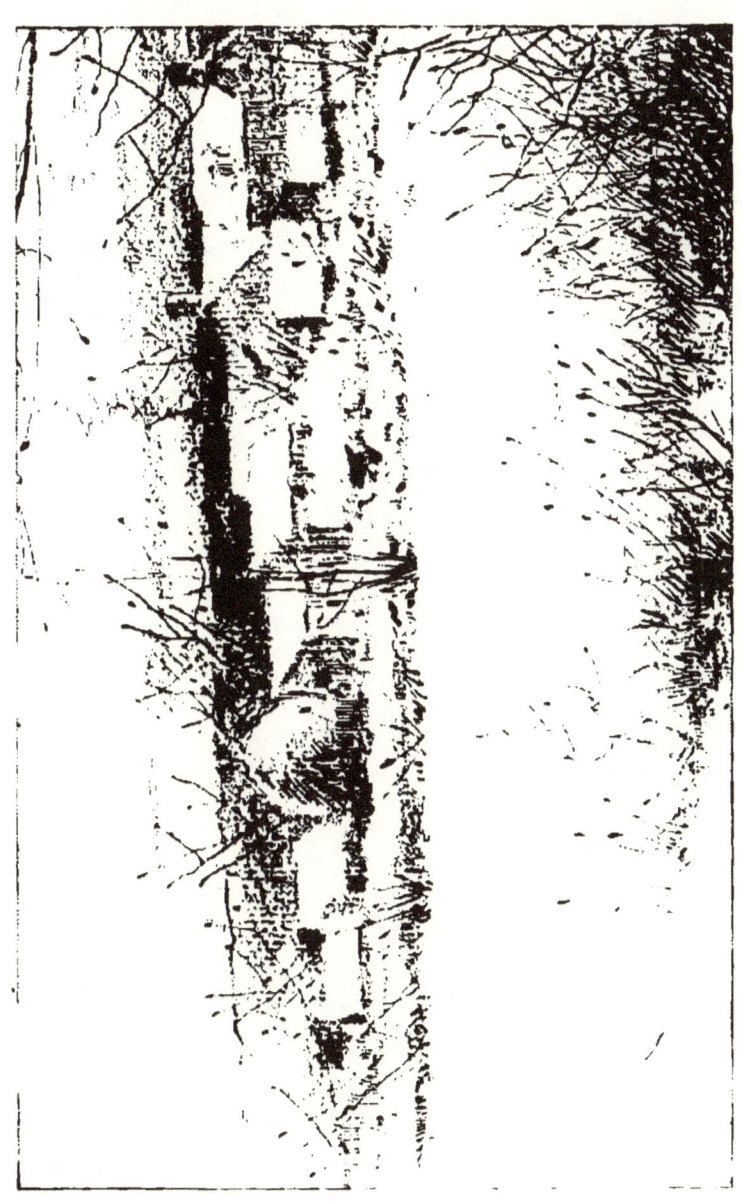

The whole imprisoned river growls below.
Loud rings the frozen earth, and, hard, reflects
A double noise; while, at his evening watch,
The village dog deters the nightly thief;
The heifer lows; the distant water-fall
Swells in the breeze; and, with the hasty
    tread
Of traveller, the hollow-sounding plain
Shakes from afar. The full ethereal round,
Infinite worlds disclosing to the view,
Shines out intensely keen; and, all one cope
Of starry glitter, glows from pole to pole.
From pole to pole the rigid influence falls,
Through the still night, incessant, heavy,
    strong,
And seizes Nature fast. It freezes on;
Till Morn, late rising o'er the drooping
    world,
Lifts her pale eye unjoyous. Then appears
The various labour of the silent night:
Prone from the dripping eave, and dumb
    cascade
Whose idle torrents only seem to roar,
The pendent icicle; the frost-work fair,

Where transient hues and fancied figures
    rise ;
Wide-spouted o'er the hill, the frozen brook,
A livid tract, cold-gleaming on the morn ;
The forest bent beneath the plumy wave ;
And by the frost refined, the whiter snow,
Incrusted hard, and sounding to the tread
Of early shepherd, as he pensive seeks
His pining flock, or from the mountain top,
Pleased with the slippery surface, swift de-
    scends.
    On blithesome frolics bent, the youthful
    swains,
While every work of man is laid at rest,
Fond o'er the river crowd, in various sport
And revelry dissolved ; where mixing glad,
Happiest of all the train, the raptured boy
Lashes the whirling top. Or, where the
    Rhine
Branched out in many a long canal extends,
From every province swarming, void of care,
Batavia rushes forth : and as they sweep,
On sounding skates, a thousand different
    ways

In circling poise, swift as the winds, along,
The then gay land is maddened all to joy.
Nor less the northern courts, wide o'er the
    snow,

Pour a new pomp. Eager, on rapid sleds,
Their vigorous youth in bold contention
    wheel
The long-resounding course. Meantime, to
    raise

The manly strife, with highly blooming
    charms,
Flushed by the season. Scandinavia's dames,
Or Russia's buxom daughters, glow around.
  Pure, quick, and sportful is the wholesome
    day ;
But soon elapsed.   The horizontal sun,
Broad o'er the south, hangs at his utmost
    noon,
And ineffectual strikes the gelid cliff :
His azure gloss the mountain still maintains,
Nor feels the feeble touch.   Perhaps the vale
Relents awhile to the reflected ray ;
Or from the forest falls the clustered snow,
Myriads of gems, that in the waving gleam
Gay-twinkle as they scatter.   Thick around
Thunders the sport of those, who with the
    gun,
And dog impatient bounding at the shot,
Worse than the season, desolate the fields ;
And, adding to the ruins of the year,
Distress the footed or the feathered game.
  But what is this? our infant Winter sinks,
Divested of his grandeur, should our eye

Astonished shoot into the frigid zone;
Where, for relentless months, continual
  Night
Holds o'er the glittering waste her starry
  reign.
  There, through the prison of unbounded
    wilds,
Barred by the hand of Nature from escape,
Wide roams the Russian exile.   Naught
  around
Strikes his sad eye, but deserts lost in snow,
And heavy-loaded groves, and solid floods,
That stretch, athwart the solitary vast,
Their icy horrors to the frozen main;
And cheerless towns far distant, never blessed,
Save when its annual course the caravan
Bends to the golden coast of rich Cathay,
With news of human-kind.   Yet there life
  glows;
Yet cherished there, beneath the shining
  waste,
The furry nations harbour: tipped with jet,
Fair ermines, spotless as the snows they
  press;

Sables, of glossy black; and dark-embrowned,
Or beauteous freaked with many a mingled
    hue,
Thousands besides, the costly pride of courts.
There, warm together pressed, the trooping
    deer
Sleep on the new-fallen snows; and, scarce
    his head
Raised o'er the heapy wreath, the branching
    elk
Lies slumbering sullen in the white abyss.
The ruthless hunter wants nor dogs nor toils,
Nor with the dread of sounding bows he
    drives
The fearful, flying race; with ponderous
    clubs,
As, weak, against the mountain-heaps they
    push
Their beating breast in vain, and piteous
    bray,
He lays them quivering on the ensanguined
    snows,
And with loud shouts rejoicing bears them
    home.

There, through the piny forest, half-absorpt,
Rough tenant of these shades, the shapeless
    bear,
With dangling ice all horrid, stalks forlorn ;
Slow-paced, and sourer as the storms increase,
He makes his bed beneath the inclement
    drift,
And, with stern patience, scorning weak com-
    plaint,
Hardens his heart against assailing want.
  Wide o'er the spacious regions of the
    north,
That see Boötes urge his tardy wain,
A boisterous race, by frosty Caurus pierced,
Who little pleasure know and fear no pain,
Prolific swarm.   They once relumed the
    flame
Of lost mankind in polished slavery sunk :
Drove martial horde on horde, with dreadful
    sweep
Resistless rushing o'er the enfeebled south,
And gave the vanquished world another form.
Not such the sons of Lapland : wisely they
Despise the insensate barbarous trade of war ;

73

They ask no more than simple Nature gives;
They love their mountains, and enjoy their
    storms.
No false desires, no pride-created wants,
Disturb the peaceful current of their time;
And, through the restless ever tortured maze
Of pleasure, or ambition, bid it rage.
Their reindeer form their riches.   These their
    tents,
Their robes, their beds, and all their homely
    wealth
Supply, their wholesome fare, and cheerful
    cups.
Obsequious at their call, the docile tribe
Yield to the sled their necks, and whirl them
    swift
O'er hill and dale, heaped into one expanse
Of marbled snow, or far as eye can sweep
With a blue crust of ice unbounded glazed.
By dancing meteors then, that ceaseless
    shake
A waving blaze refracted o'er the heavens,
And vivid moons, and stars that keener play
With double lustre from the radiant waste,

Even in the depth of polar night, they find
A wondrous day — enough to light the chase,
Or guide their daring steps to Finland fairs.
Wished Spring returns; and, from the hazy
     south,

While dim Aurora slowly moves before,
The welcome sun, just verging up at first,
By small degrees extends the swelling curve;
Till seen at last for gay rejoicing months,
Still round and round his spiral course he
     winds,   **75**

And as he nearly dips his flaming orb,
Wheels up again, and reascends the sky.
In that glad season, from the lakes and
floods,
Where pure Niemi's fairy mountains rise,
And, fringed with roses, Tenglio rolls his
stream,
They draw the copious fry. With these, at
eve.
They, cheerful, loaded to their tents repair;
Where, all day long in useful cares employed,
Their kind unblemished wives the fire pre-
pare.
Thrice happy race! by poverty secured
From legal plunder and rapacious power;
In whom fell interest never yet has sown
The seeds of vice; whose spotless swains
ne'er knew
Injurious deed, nor, blasted by the breath
Of faithless love, their blooming daughters
woe.
  Still pressing on, beyond Tornéa's lake,
And Hecla flaming through a waste of snow,
And farthest Greenland, to the pole itself,

Winter.

Where, failing gradual, life at length goes out,
The Muse expands her solitary flight;
And, hovering o'er the wild stupendous scene,
Beholds new seas beneath another sky.
Throned in his palace of cerulean ice,
Here Winter holds his unrejoicing court;
And through his airy hall the loud misrule
Of driving tempest is forever heard:
Here the grim tyrant meditates his wrath;
Here arms his winds with all-subduing frost;
Moulds his fierce hail, and treasures up his
    snows,
With which he now oppresses half the globe.
  Thence winding eastward to the Tartar's
    coast.
She sweeps the howling margin of the main;
Where undissolving, from the first of time,
Snows swell on snows amazing to the sky;
And icy mountains high on mountains piled,
Seem to the shivering sailor from afar
Shapeless and white, an atmosphere of clouds,
Projected huge and horrid, o'er the surge,
Alps frown on Alps; or rushing hideous
    down,

As if old chaos was again returned,
Wide-rend the deep, and shake the solid pole.
Ocean itself no longer can resist
The binding fury: but, in all its rage
Of tempest taken by the boundless frost,
Is many a fathom to the bottom chained,
And bid to roar no more: a bleak expanse,
Shagged o'er with wavy rocks, cheerless, and
    void
Of every life, that from the dreary months
Flies conscious southward. Miserable they,
Who, here entangled in the gathering ice,
Take their last look of the descending sun;
While, full of death, and fierce with tenfold
    frost,
The long, long night, incumbent o'er their
    heads,
Falls horrible. Such was the Briton's fate,
As with first prow (what have not Britons
    dared!)
He for the passage sought, attempted since
So much in vain, and seeming to be shut
By jealous Nature with eternal bars.
In these fell regions, in Arzina caught,

And to the stony deep his idle ship
Immediate sealed, he, with his hapless crew.
Each full exerted at his several task,
Froze into statues ; to the cordage glued

The sailor, and the pilot to the helm.
  Hard by these shores. where scarce his
    freezing stream
Rolls the wild Oby. live the last of men ;

And half-enlivened by the distant sun,
That rears and ripens man, as well as plants,
Here human nature wears its rudest form.
Deep from the piercing season sunk in caves,
Here by dull fires, and with unjoyous cheer,
They waste the tedious gloom. Immersed
  in furs,
Doze the gross race : nor sprightly jest, nor
  song,
Nor tenderness, they know ; nor aught of life,
Beyond the kindred bears that stalk without :
Till morn at length, her roses drooping all,
Sheds a long twilight brightening o'er their
  fields,
And calls the quivered savage to the chase.
 What cannot active government perform,
New-moulding man? Wide-stretching from
  these shores,
A people savage from remotest time,
A huge neglected empire, one vast mind,
By Heaven inspired, from Gothic darkness
  called.
Immortal Peter! first of monarchs! he
His stubborn country tamed, her rocks, her
  fens.   82

Her floods, her seas, her ill-submitting sons;
And while the fierce barbarian he subdued,
To more exalted soul he raised the man.
Ye shades of ancient heroes, ye who toiled
Through long successive ages to build up
A labouring plan of state, behold at once
The wonder done! behold the matchless
    prince!
Who left his native throne, where reigned till
    then
A mighty shadow of unreal power;
Who greatly spurned the slothful pomp of
    courts;
And roaming every land, in every port
His sceptre laid aside, with glorious hand
Unwearied plying the mechanic tool,
Gathered the seeds of trade, of useful arts,
Of civil wisdom, and of martial skill.
Charged with the stores of Europe home he
    goes:
Then cities rise amid the illumined waste;
O'er joyless deserts smiles the rural reign;
Far-distant flood to flood is social joined:
The astonished Euxine hears the Baltic roar;

Proud navies ride on seas that never foamed
With daring keel before; and armies stretch
Each way their dazzling files, repressing here
The frantic Alexander of the north,
And awing there stern Othman's shrinking
    sons.
Sloth flies the land, and ignorance, and vice,
Of old dishonour proud: it glows around,
Taught by the royal hand that roused the
    whole.
One scene of arts, of arms, of rising trade:
For what his wisdom planned, and power en-
    forced,
More potent still, his great example showed.
  Muttering, the winds at eve, with blunted
    point,
Blow hollow-blustering from the south. Sub-
    dued,
The frost resolves into a trickling thaw.
Spotted the mountains shine; loose sleet de-
    scends,
And floods the country round. The rivers
    swell,
Of bonds impatient. Sudden from the hills,

Winter.

O'er rocks and woods, in broad brown cataracts,
A thousand snow-fed torrents shoot at once :
And, where they rush, the wide-resounding
    plain

Is left one slimy waste.   Those sullen seas,
That washed the ungenial pole, will rest no
    more
Beneath the shackles of the mighty north :
But, rousing all their waves, resistless heave.

85

And hark! the lengthening roar continuous
    runs
Athwart the rifted deep: at once it bursts,
And piles a thousand mountains to the
    clouds.
Ill fares the bark with trembling wretches
    charged.
That, tossed amid the floating fragments,
    moors
Beneath the shelter of an icy isle.
While night o'erwhelms the sea, and horror
    looks
More horrible.   Can human force endure
The assembled mischiefs that besiege them
    round?
Heart-gnawing hunger, fainting weariness,
The roar of winds and waves, the crush of
    ice.
Now ceasing, now renewed with louder rage,
And in dire echoes bellowing round the main.
More to embroil the deep. Leviathan
And his unwieldy train, in dreadful sport,
Tempest the loosened brine; while, through
    the gloom,

Far from the bleak inhospitable shore,
Loading the winds, is heard the hungry howl
Of famished monsters, there awaiting wrecks.
Yet Providence, that ever-waking eye,
Looks down with pity on the feeble toil
Of mortals lost to hope, and lights them safe
Through all this dreary labyrinth of fate.
   'T is done! — dread Winter spreads his
     latest glooms,
And reigns, tremendous, o'er the conquered
     year.
How dead the vegetable kingdom lies!
How dumb the tuneful! Horror wide extends
His desolate domain. Behold, fond man!
See here thy pictured life : pass some few
     years,
Thy flowering Spring, thy Summer's ardent
     strength,
Thy sober Autumn, fading into age,
And pale, concluding Winter comes at last,
And shuts the scene Ah! whither now are
     fled
Those dreams of greatness? those unsolid
     hopes

Of happiness? those longings after fame?
Those restless cares? those busy, bustling
    days?
Those gay-spent, festive nights? those veer-
    ing thoughts,
Lost between good and ill, that shared thy
    life?
All now are vanished! virtue sole survives, —
Immortal, never-failing friend of man,
His guide to happiness on high.   And see!
'T is come, the glorious morn! the second
    birth
Of heaven and earth! awakening Nature
    hears
The new creating word, and starts to life,
In every heightened form, from pain and
    death
Forever free.   The great eternal scheme,
Involving all, and in a perfect whole
Uniting, as the prospect wider spreads,
To reason's eye, refined, clears up apace.
Ye vainly wise! ye blind presumptuous! now,
Confounded in the dust, adore that power
And Wisdom oft arraigned: see now the
    cause   90

Why unassuming Worth in secret lived.
And died neglected: why the good man's
    share

In life was gall and bitterness of soul:
Why the lone widow and her orphans pined
In starving solitude; while Luxury.
In palaces. lay straining her low thought,

To form unreal wants: why heaven-born
    Truth,
And Moderation fair, wore the red marks
Of superstition's scourge: why licensed Pain,
That cruel spoiler, that embosomed foe,
Embittered all our bliss. Ye good, dis-
    tressed!
Ye noble few! who here unbending stand
Beneath life's pressure, yet bear up awhile,
And what your bounded view — which only
    saw
A little part — deemed evil, is no more:
The storms of wintry time will quickly pass,
And one unbounded Spring encircle all.

92